JUSTIN MORGAN HAD A HORSE

JUSTIN MORGAN HAD A HORSE

by Marguerite Henry

ILLUSTRATIONS BY WESLEY DENNIS

WILCOX & FOLLETT CO.
CHICAGO

First Printing 1945
Second Printing 1946
Third Printing 1947
Fourth Printing 1948

THIS is the story of a common ordinary little work horse which turned out to be the father of a famous family of American horses. He lived in the Green Mountain country of Vermont in the days when our country was growing up. In fact, he helped it grow up. He dragged logs and cleared the land. He helped build the first log huts. He helped build bridges and cut roads through the wilderness.

There was not much that this courageous little horse could not do. He labored hard by day. At the end of the day he took part in races and pulling bees. He could walk faster, trot faster, run faster, and pull heavier logs than any horse in Vermont.

Today his descendants, known as Morgan horses, are famous throughout the world. Yet nobody knows whether the first Morgan's parents were British or French or Dutch. And nobody really cares. As Joel Goss said, "Come to think of it, he's like us. He's American. That's what he is. American!"

Ebenezer and Little Bub

The little reddish-brown colt stopped nibbling grass. He lifted his head and sniffed the wind. His pink nose trembled.

A man and a boy were coming up the road.

He sniffed again. Quick little sniffs. These strangers must have journeyed a long way. Their man-smell was almost blotted with dust.

Now the colt whinnied sharply. In an instant, a big colt, perhaps a year older, stopped grazing. He stopped so suddenly that it seemed almost as if his name had been called out. He trotted over to the little colt and nuzzled him gently. Then his ears pricked. Now he, too, knew that strangers were coming up the road.

The man was lean-faced and tall. He was at the fence now, his arms resting on the top rail. The boy at his side was barefoot. His blue linsey-woolsey shirt was faded and torn, and his breeches, held up by a string of cowhide, were gray with dust. His hair was stubbly and straw-colored, like a cut-over field of wheat. Everything about the boy looked dry and parched. Everything except his eyes. These peered over the fence with a lively curiosity.

[7]

"We're here, Joel," said the man, with a little sigh. "We can put our bundles down and rest a spell before we go in."

The boy had not heard. He just stood there, staring at the colts as if he had never seen their like before. "The little one," he breathed, "I could gentle him, I could."

Just then a door slammed shut, and a farmer stepped out into the morning sun.

"Halloo there, Abner Beane!" called the man at the fence.

"Morning!" replied the farmer peering out under his hand. And then as he walked over to eye the newcomers he caught his breath.

"Great Jumping Jehoshaphat!" he whistled. "If it ain't Justin Morgan, schoolmaster and singing teacher! Why, I'm as pleasured to see you as a dog with two tails. And who's the young feller here?"

"This young lad," replied the schoolmaster as he put his hand on the boy's shoulder, "this young lad is my friend, Joel Goss. I boarded with his parents last school year." Turning to the boy he said, "Joel, I want you to meet an old friend."

Joel's eyes were fastened on the colts. Reluctantly he turned and faced Farmer Beane. He had never been introduced before. It made him blush to the roots of his sunburnt hair.

"Where in tarnation you two come from? You hain't come all the ways from Randolph, Vermont, to West Springfield, Massachusetts?" asked the farmer.

Justin Morgan nodded.

"Sakes alive! You must be all tuckered out. Why it's over a hundred miles down here. Didn't walk the whole way, I hope."

The schoolmaster took off his hat and ran his fingers through graying hair. "No, Abner," he said wearily. "We came part way with Lem Tubbs and his team of oxen."

"Well, let's not stand here a-gabbing. Come in. Come in. The woman'll give us some hot johnnycake and coffee. I'll bet Joel here could do with some vittles. He's skinny as a fiddle string. Come in, come in. By and by we can visit."

All during the conversation the colts had been inching closer and closer. Now they were snuffing at Farmer Beane's pockets, and tugging at his sleeves.

"These tarnal creatures just love to be the whole show," chuckled the farmer, as he reached into his pocket. "If I don't bring 'em their maple sugar each morning, the day don't begin right for them—or me either."

Justin Morgan steadied himself against the fence. "Before Joel and I eat your victuals," he said, "it seems as though I should tell you I've come to collect the money you owed me when I moved away to Vermont."

There was a long minute of silence. It was so still that the colts munching their sugar seemed to be very noisy about it. Joel thought of the bright red apple he had eaten last night. He wished now that he had saved it for the colts.

Finally the farmer said, "You have come a terrible long way, Justin, and 'tis hard for me to disappoint you. But me and the woman have had nothing but trouble. Last year my cows got in the cornfield and et theirselves sick and died. The year before that the corn was too burned to harvest. I just hain't got the money," he added limply.

The schoolmaster's shoulders slumped until his homespun jacket looked big and loose, as if it had been made for someone else. "I'd set such store on getting the money," was all he said.

"But I ain't one to forget my debts," the farmer explained more cheerfully. "I've a mind to give you a colt instead of the cash."

Joel wheeled around to see if Farmer Beane was in earnest.

"Now this big feller, this Ebenezer," he was saying, "is a creature with get-up-and-get. He'll be a go-ahead horse. It would be hard to find a sensibler animal if you looked all up and down the Connecticut valley. Besides, he's halterbroke. He'd be *just* the horse to ride to school."

The schoolmaster slowly shook his head. "It would be just another mouth to feed."

"Why, bless my breeches," laughed Abner heartily. "I bet you could sell him before you run up a feed bill. All the river folk got their eye on him. He'll fetch a pocket of money. Maybe twice as much as I owe you!"

Justin Morgan studied his dust-covered boots as if he did not want to look at Ebenezer at all.

"And now for the premium," the farmer added as an afterthought, "I'll give you Little Bub here too. 'Course he ain't the colt that Ebenezer is. He's just a little mite of a thing. But there's *something* about those two. They stay together as snug as two teaspoons. Scarcely ever do you see one of the creatures alone. Eb's kind of like a mother to Bub. Why, I've seen Bub nip Ebenezer on the flanks, and that big colt *knew* it was just in fun! He'd turn right round and lick the little one. You'd actually think the colt was his!"

Master Morgan laughed a dry sort of laugh, like wind rustling through a cornfield. "I don't need two horses any more than I need water in my hat! It would be just two more mouths to feed."

"Reckon I could feed them?" offered Joel timidly.

The schoolmaster's eyes smiled down at Joel. "In the hills of Vermont, lad," he said, "farmers want big handsome oxen. Not undersized horses."

The smaller colt stood so close to the fence now that Joel reached out and gently touched his brown nose. It felt like plush.

"Ee-magine that!" clucked the farmer. "The little nipper didn't even buck. This lad's got a way about him. Wouldn't wonder if he could gentle the creature."

Now Farmer Beane picked up Ebenezer's feet, one by one. "Look ahere, Justin, you know the good from the bad. See how mannerly he is!"

Next he pressed Ebenezer's muscles, and lifted his upper lip to show the strong teeth.

Then he turned to the little colt. "Bub's only pint size," he said,

"but he's got a good disposition. Except when he sees a dog. He just can't *abide* dogs! They make him mad as a hornet. He strikes out at them with his feet, and squeals, and chases them until they go lickety-split for home with their tails tucked clean underneath their bellies."

"It's kind of you to offer both colts, Abner, but you keep Little Bub. In Vermont I can sell Ebenezer, but the little creature would be just a worry to me."

The boy and the schoolmaster saw no more of the colts that day. After a good breakfast served up by Mistress Beane, they went into West Springfield on business. The colts, meanwhile, were busy with their own affairs—galloping from one end of the pasture to the other, rolling in the cool grass, leaping and pawing at butterflies and pieces of thistledown.

A Fuzzy Shadow

Next morning when the grass was still wet with dew and the moon hung like a white ball in the sky, Ebenezer and Little Bub were turned out to pasture. The cool morning air set them to prancing. They raced round and round in a wide circle, then tossed their heads in the air and whinnied for joy.

Before long, the farmer, with Master Morgan and Joel, came out of the house. While the men talked, Joel made his way over to the far end of the meadow where the colts were frolicking. Then, standing very still, he took two apples from inside his shirt and offered one on the palm of each hand.

Ebenezer eyed the boy for only a moment. Then he came forward and neatly lifted an apple off Joel's hand. Little Bub, however, danced away and snorted. But when the boy made no move he became curious. Besides, he could hear Ebenezer crunching the apple, and he could smell its sweetness. He came a step closer, then another, and another. At last his soft lips touched Joel's hand. Joel could feel the

funny little whiskers. It gave him gooseflesh all over. Then the colt took the apple, and in that little moment boy and animal were friends.

"I wish it was you that was coming along," Joel whispered in the colt's ear. "Ebenezer's big and fine, but you and me—we could grow big together!"

Master Morgan came up very quietly now and slipped a halter around Ebenezer's head. Gently he led him through the gate, then reached over the fence to shake hands with Farmer Beane.

"I'm grateful to you for Ebenezer," he said. "Maybe he'll be worth his salt after all."

"And I'm obliged to you for crossing off the debt, Justin. 'Twas extraordinary nice of you to put it in writing. I always did say you was the handsomest writer and the best singer in the whole state of Massachusetts."

Without a word of command, the little colt had turned out of the gate too. In the gray morning light he looked like a fuzzy shadow of Ebenezer.

"Hey, Justin!" called the farmer. "The little one is coming along, too."

Joel was almost afraid to breathe. He looked neither to the right nor to the left. His bare feet sank noiselessly into the dust. "Please God," he whispered, "don't let Little Bub turn back. Please God, *don't let him turn back.*"

At first the small colt threw his head high and investigated the wind with all manner of snuffings and snortings. Then his delicate ears pointed this way and that to gather in the new strange sounds. At last he switched his black curly tail. "I'm coming along!" he said, plainer than if he had talked.

Joel could hold his excitement no longer. He let out a great sigh of happiness. There was no mistaking it now. Little Bub was his! At least for the long journey home the colt was his.

They were scarcely out upon the high road when Master Morgan began talking. Schoolteaching was in his blood, and he could not help instructing along the way.

"Well, Joel," he began in his first-day-of-school voice, "we have two new pupils today, and I'm in favor of making this a skylarking trip. Now if we go along at a steady pace, we might reach the village of Chicopee before the sun is over our heads. That's the spot where the Chicopee River swings into the great Connecticut River. We'll cross a bridge there too."

He turned to look at the colts. "You two little shavers ever been over a bridge? Like as not. But you'll admire the sound of your hoofs clattering over the wood. See if you don't."

From the very first, the colts liked the schoolmaster's voice. It seemed part of the wind and the river. And the way he looked at them when he talked—why it was as if they were all gentlemen making a pilgrimage together!

"Along about twilight," the master went on, "we should be near enough to Hadley Falls to feel the spray of it on our faces. We'll have

our suppers there. Joel and I will fish for trout while you two nippers have your fill of the delicious grass that grows on the banks. And I wouldn't wonder but what an obliging farmer will have a bag of oats to trade for the writing of a letter or the singing of an anthem. Then we'll bed down under the stars and let the music of the falls and the warmth of our campfire put us to sleep."

Ebenezer whinnied, and Little Bub added his ·high notes which ended in a low rumble. Joel laughed. "Bub's trying to act like a grown-up horse," he said.

Occasionally they passed an oxcart loaded down with grain or flax, and the driver would stop and chat awhile.

"Fine big colt you got there," the driver would usually say. "But that little bugger don't look like he'll amount to much."

Always it was the same. *Every*one admired Ebenezer. The traveling cobbler who joined up with them one day even offered to buy Ebenezer in trade for his lapstone and awl. But Master Morgan needed cobbler's tools even less than he needed a horse.

It was almost a month's trip from West Springfield, Massachusetts, to Randolph, Vermont. The schoolmaster had to stop often to rest in the shade. This gave the colts a chance to roll in the grass and scratch their backs. It gave them time to plunge their muzzles into cool streams. And it gave Joel an opportunity to set his bundle of clothes on Little Bub to get him acquainted with the feel of something on his back.

Sometimes, when they came to a tidy farmhouse, the air would be laden with delicious smells—the sweet spiciness of gingerbread and applejohn baking, and the steaming fragrance of pork pie. Joel and the schoolmaster would follow the scent like bird dogs after quail. Usually it led them past a little flower garden and around to some friendly kitchen door.

There the schoolmaster removed his hat. Then, with his eyes on the smoke curling from the chimney, he would sing:

> So pilgrims on the scorching sand,
> Beneath a burning sky
> Long for a cooling stream at hand;
> And they must drink or die.

Before he reached the second stanza the farmer's wife and children would be out on their doorstep, listening eagerly to the words and the tune. Sometimes Joel sang along with the master. And every now and again Ebenezer sounded his bugle notes, and Little Bub rumbled along with a low obbligato. This sent the children into peals of laughter.

Suddenly the farmwife would think of her baking, and send her eldest in to mind it. Then she would not hear of the master and the boy starting out again until they had a hot meal inside them, and a cold snack to take along. Even the colts were usually watered and fed.

"It was kinder nice," the wife would say as she watched the boy and the schoolmaster enjoy her pork pie, "to listen to hymn music without its being Sabbath day."

When the little procession left, often as not the children would walk part way, teasing the master for more songs.

"Joel, of course, knows," Master Morgan would confide to them, "but I may as well tell you younglings that I composed these anthems myself. And nothing pleasures me more than to sing them."

But there were days when the schoolmaster did not sing at all—days when the only sounds were the soft thud of hoofs and Joel talking to the little colt. The thing that Joel never dreamed *could* happen *was* happening. The colt was answering in funny little whickers, as if he agreed with all Joel said.

At the first sign of dusk Master Morgan and the big colt would grow uneasy. Their eyes searched the shadows for wildcats, and Ebenezer's nostrils flared to catch the scent of them. Most of the night—when he was not tending the fire—the schoolmaster sat cross-legged, his elbows on his knees, his head resting in his hands. Ebenezer dozed standing up. The sleep of both man and horse was fitful and troubled.

They started at the slightest noise—an acorn falling, the pitapat of rabbit's feet across dry leaves, the faint whistle of a peeper frog, the gnawing of beavers, the piping squeak of field mice, the mournful cry of a hoot owl.

Joel and Bub, however, were lulled by the little voices of the night. The colt lay stretched out on his side, and gradually the boy edged nearer and nearer until by morning he was curled snug against the little colt's back. It felt warm and furry, and Bub did not seem to mind.

Daylight found these two eager and ready for new adventures. Whether rain or hot sunshine beat down on their heads, their dispositions were equally cheerful. Steep, stony trails, skimpy food at odd hours, nothing discouraged them.

When they crossed the Massachusetts state line into Vermont, the schoolmaster seemed to gain new strength. He could not stop talking about the magic of the mountains. "You see," he said, "Vermont is named for its mountains, *vert* for green and *mont* for mountain.

"The first settlers had a regular ceremony when they named these mountains," he explained. "A minister and a loyal band of men climbed to the very top of Mount Pisgah. From there the whole territory spread out before them like a carpet of green, with silver threads where the rivers wound."

Then in his soft husky voice, Master Morgan recited: "*I will lift up mine eyes unto the hills from whence cometh my help.*"

The colts looked off in the direction of the mountains as if they, too, admired their dark green splendor. But the schoolmaster did not know that horses are unable to see very far ahead. He never suspected that

[23]

his beloved mountains were only a hazy blur to them. In fact, Ebenezer towered so big that about all Little Bub could see was the switching tail ahead of him. That was good enough, however. It comforted him. Everything was all right as long as he could tag along after his big friend.

Horse-Trader Hawkes

On and on they went, past tiny towns perched on hilltops or nestled in the crook of some stream. Nearly always a church spire rose from the cluster of homes and sharpened itself against the sky.

They passed wheat fields, and fields of Indian corn with yellow squash planted between the rows.

They saw pigs wearing great wood collars to keep them from straying, and fat bears eating berries, and brown weasels scuttling in the underbrush. They saw small lakes, like polished mirrors, and fishermen in boats, and white-tailed deer at the water's edge.

They heard the bleating of sheep and the jingle of their bells. They heard wild geese honking, and beavers slapping their tails against the water, and blue jays screaming. They listened to the military music of waterfalls and the cradlesong of brooks.

They clattered over covered bridges with the printed warning:

Walk Your Horses

"That's all we've *been* doing!" Master Morgan would smile wearily.

They waited for ferries to take them across swift-flowing rivers. Ebenezer, it was plain to see, was struck with terror at sight of a ferry. He had to be petted and coaxed to get on. Then he stood stiff-legged and scared until the trip was over. But Little Bub walked up the runway almost gaily. One ferryman nudged Master Morgan and laughed, "If it was just me alone to consider, I'd let the lad and the runt go over for two pence apiece, same's a goat!"

They walked through deep grass and across broken country. They climbed up and up steep hills. At the summits, the schoolmaster would stop to admire the country spread out at his feet. "Mother Nature is an orderly creature," he would say. Then he would hum little hymn tunes until he felt rested again

On the Sabbath day they never traveled at all, because there was a law in Vermont forbidding it. Instead, the schoolmaster and the boy went to the nearest meetinghouse. The colts meanwhile were tied to the hitching rack outside. They looked little and frisky alongside the huge oxen and work horses.

The sermon, drifting out of the doorway, sounded to the animals like the faraway droning of bumblebees. Soon they were nodding and dozing in the warm sunshine until they heard the preacher bring his fist down with a bang. Little Bub always snorted then and gave his high neigh, with that funny rumble afterward. Inside their box pew Joel and the schoolmaster exchanged sly glances, never smiling openly —for the tithingman stood ready with his staff to tap anyone who acted unseemly on the Sabbath.

Between morning and afternoon service the worshipers often invited Master Morgan and Joel to join them in the noontide meal.

"We figure you folks come a-traveling a good long ways," some motherly person would say. "You must be a mite hungry."

With smiles of anticipation, the schoolmaster and the boy followed the little flock as it spread out under the elm trees like hungry sparrows. Then from picnic hampers came the drumsticks and wings of cold gander, thick slices of ham, homemade cheese, and brown-bread sandwiches filled with rich layers of apple butter.

Meanwhile the work horses at the hitching rack were made to share their oats with the colts.

It was growing toward pumpkin time when they came to the junction of the Connecticut and White Rivers. "At last! At last we leave the Connecticut!" the schoolmaster rejoiced. "When the Indians named it the Long River, they were right as a bonnet in church!"

The nearer they came to Randolph, however, the deeper grew the worry lines on Master Morgan's brow. Forests were thinning out now, and houses huddled along the east branch of the White River.

"Chimney smoke and candlelight look mighty inviting to me," the schoolmaster sighed, "and I don't know but what I could do with some hasty pudding and tea. What do you say, Joel, if we stay the night with my sister Eunice? Then we can see what neighbor Hawkes

[27]

thinks of our colts. He's as good a judge of horseflesh as there is, and a sharp trader. He may even want to buy the colts."

Fear struck at Joel's heart. "Couldn't you just sell Ebenezer?" he asked quickly. "Little Bub probably wouldn't fetch much anyway."

Neighbor Hawkes was at breakfast when Master Morgan, Joel, and their two colts appeared early the next morning. He came out onto the stoop, wiping his mouth with the back of his hand.

"Jumping Aunt Minnie!" he gulped. "We thought you two was never coming back, and here you be with two colts to boot."

"What do you think of them?" asked Master Morgan, nervously.

Hawkes squinted one eye. He approached the animals cautiously, taking care to keep out of kicking range. He circled one at a time. Then he stood with his legs braced far apart.

"Well now, Justin," he drawled as he scratched the stubble on his chin, "the big feller looks just fair to middling—just fair to middling, I'd say. But that little cob—he won't be worth no more than ten dollars, even when he's grown up. Legs too short for one thing. Just not strung up right. Now you've asked, and I've give it to you straight."

"Wouldn't want to buy the little one for trading?" Master Morgan suggested.

Hawkes laughed, a loud laugh. "Me? I'd sooner buy that weathervane horse on yonder barn!"

Little Bub snorted fiercely, as if he wanted to blow out all smell of this man Hawkes. Even Ebenezer laid back his ears.

By ginger! thought Joel. Eb and Bub are good judges, too! And he laughed softly to himself.

Bound Boy

The sun was almost overhead when Joel spied the sugar maples shading his own log house, and the sheep browsing in his front yard. All through Randolph and along the river road he and the schoolmaster had been delayed with questions about Ebenezer and Little Bub. Now Joel had an uneasy feeling that news of the colts had trickled on ahead of them.

"Could be!" reasoned Joel. "Else why is Pa blocking the doorway, his feet planted solid, like the ram's when he's fixing to butt?"

The next thing Joel knew, a slight figure had darted around his father, and was holding him close.

"Ma!" cried Joel. "We're home!"

Ma did not need to be told. Her eyes were flooded with happiness. She felt of Joel to make sure that he was all in one piece. Then, when she was quite satisfied, she turned to Master Morgan. "You look peaked, Master, but WELCOME HOME! The *four* of you!" she added with a smile for the colts, and then a worried glance toward the door.

Mister Goss had not moved. He stood rigid and glowering. Only a disrespectful breeze played with his brown beard.

In dismay Joel led Ebenezer and Little Bub to the empty shed behind the house. He took as long as possible to make the creatures comfortable.

"It was my doing, bringing the colts home," the schoolmaster was explaining as Joel entered the kitchen. "I calculate to sell them soon." Then, stiffly, he climbed the ladder to his room in the loft, and closed the trap door behind him.

Mister Goss's eyes were blazing now.

"Ma!" he thundered. "Joel, here, had a finger in this, but I don't aim to play nursemaid to two colts. I'm through having horses on the place, I tell you. Recollect that last colt? No sooner do I have him broke than he stumbles and breaks a leg and I got to shoot him. What in tunket they think I am? Don't they know oats come high? By thunder!" he exploded, pounding his fist on the table until the dishes jumped. "I won't have it!"

"Now don't get riled, Pa," soothed Mrs. Goss, wondering if there were enough pumpkin pies to satisfy Joel and the master.

"That ain't all!" roared Mister Goss. "Boarding the schoolmaster's got to stop too. High time he found a new place, and high time our Joel learnt a trade." Suddenly he looked up as if he were greatly pleased with the idea. He stopped bellowing and now his voice wheedled.

"I heerd that Mister Chase needs an apprentice," he said, thumping Joel on the back, "and here's his boy."

Joel thought the noon meal would never end. Even his favorite pumpkin pie was flannel in his mouth. Every spoonful stuck in his throat, like the time he had quinsy.

At last Pa shoved his plate aside and motioned Joel to follow him. Without a word they walked out into the afternoon sunshine and set off for Chase's Inn.

Only once did Joel turn back. His mother, looking very small, was waving her apron at him, a flag of courage.

It was less than a quarter of a mile to Chase's Inn, but to Joel it seemed longer than the whole trip from Massachusetts to Vermont! Once he thought he heard Ebenezer neighing and Little Bub sending forth his high notes which died out in that funny rumble.

As luck would have it, Mister Chase was adding up his accounts on the bar counter when Joel and his father walked in.

Mister Goss wasted no time on the weather. He came straight to the point. "I'd admire," he said, "to have you apprentice my Joel until he's twenty-one. With a sawmill and an inn to tend, you need a stout lad to help you. Joel, here, will be handy as the pocket on your coat!"

The miller's eyes lit with interest. Only this morning he had gotten a big order from the West Indies for barrel staves and hoops. Besides, Mistress Chase had been growing snappish of late. A likely lad—one who could buckle right down to work—might make things easier. Almost greedily he drew up the papers, promising to give Joel bed, board, and learning—and two suits of clothes besides. In return, Joel was to obey his commands and never leave the inn without permission. Both men signed the papers, each looking mightily pleased over the deal.

"How does it feel to be a bound boy?" laughed Miller Chase as he tweaked Joel's ear.

Joel turned white. He felt as if his own body was going through the sawmill, being cut into little pieces. Who would there be now to take care of Little Bub?

On the night before he was sent to live with Miller Chase, Justin Morgan called him into his small garret room. Spread out on the feather bed were his goose-quill pens, his inkhorn, the shiny hourglass, the brass candle snuffer—all the treasures which had made the garret room seem beautiful to Joel.

The schoolmaster cleared a space on the bed for the boy to sit down. Then he went on with his packing, talking as he worked.

"Two good things happened to me today," he smiled. "The Jenks family has agreed to board me, and I've found an honest horse dealer."

"You hain't!" cried Joel in alarm.

"Oh, Joel! I thought you were all over saying 'hain't!'"

"But the little colt—he's not sold?"

The schoolmaster laughed. "I've a good home for Ebenezer, but everywhere I try to sell Little Bub the answer is the same. 'Too small! Too small! And besides,' they say, 'the creature isn't even broken to saddle or harness!'"

Joel leaned forward eagerly. He thought he could guess what the schoolmaster had in mind.

"Now what I ask of you is this, Joel—"

"Yes?"

"Do you think you could gentle Little Bub?"

Could he gentle Little Bub! Had he thought of anything else, awake or asleep?

"After watching Pa do it ever since I was a baby?" he asked, his eyes shiny. " 'Course I could!"

Then suddenly all the eagerness faded. "You mean," he spoke slowly, "you mean I'm to gentle him—for someone else?"

"That's what I mean, lad. We are both fonder of Little Bub than men should be of any beast; but I have debts to pay, and I must pay them before I die. I need your help, Joel. Will you shake hands, man to man?"

The boy hesitated for one instant. Then he put his hand into the thin, dry one of the schoolmaster.

"I've been to see Miller Chase," the schoolmaster went on in a more cheerful tone, "and he plans to send you to night school. I wonder," he said as he wrapped a faded waistcoat about his reading boards and songbooks, "I wonder if you would like to spend an hour with the colt each night after lessons?"

"In the dark?" questioned Joel.

Justin Morgan snuffed out the tallow candle. Then he threw open the shutters and drew the boy to the gable window. The moon was three quarters full. It sifted through the trees and spattered the yard with a magical white light.

Joel let out a whistle of joy.

"For two weeks," Master Morgan said, "there will be light enough for *you* to see. Horses, you know, can see quite well in the dark."

Little Bub Is Rented Out

Never was a colt so willing to be gentled. After but two lessons, he wore a halter as if it were part of him. Like his forelock. Or his tail.

Next Joel tried the harness, and slipped a bit between his nippers and his back teeth. Bub hated the bit. He did not mind rope or leather things, but this iron was cold and frightening.

One night Joel warmed the bit in his hands, and from then on, the colt accepted it without even jerking.

Whenever Bub behaved well, Joel let him bury his nose in a bucket of oats—all the while telling him what a fine, smart horse he was. "You're my reddish-brown stallion," he would say. "Soon you'll be *big* for your size! And then you've got to be so smart and willing that even an ornery man will have no excuse to touch a whip to you. I couldn't abide that!" he added, his fists doubled.

Some nights Joel fastened a horn lantern to an old two-wheeled cart of his father's. Then, filling the cart with stones for weight, he would drive the horse over the rolling hills. Some nights he rode bareback. He practiced pulling the colt up short. He practiced walking him,

trotting him, racing him. Often they would travel ten miles in an evening.

Late on one of these evenings Joel burst into the schoolhouse so full of laughter he could scarcely talk.

The children were gone, and the boy's laughter was so hearty that the schoolmaster joined in without knowing why.

Between spasms, Joel managed to gasp, "You should have seed that little hound-dog run!"

"What little hound-dog?"

"Why Abel Hooper's," giggled Joel, bursting into fresh laughter. "He comes a-tearing out the gate and begins yammering at Little Bub and nipping his forelegs. Oh ho, ho, ho!"

"What did Bub do?"

"What did he *do*?" shrieked Joel. "Why he sprung forward like a cat outen a bag. And that idiot hound was too muddled to go home. He turned tail and streaked down the road with Bub after him."

Joel had to wipe away his tears before he could go on. "Finally," he chuckled, "the hound got so beat out I took pity on him and reined in. Why the way Little Bub can climb hills," breathed Joel, "it's like he had wings!"

When Mister Goss discovered Joel training the colt, he was furious at first. Then he boasted and bragged about it at Chase's Inn: "All that boy knows about horses he got from me!"

But the truth of the matter was that in watching his father train a colt, Joel had learned what not to do, as well as what to do. While his father could break a horse in a matter of hours, his horses often seemed broken in spirit, too. The boy was determined that this should not happen to his colt. And it had not. Little Bub's eyes were still dancy. He still tossed his mane and nosed the sky. He still had a frisky look about him. No, he had lost none of his spirit.

The moon waned and became full again. Not once, but many times. For months the schoolmaster said no more about selling the colt. And about the time when Joel began to think that Little Bub might be his forever, a man came to call on the schoolmaster. He was Ezra Fisk, a new settler.

"I've been watching a lad drive a smallish horse in the moonlight," Mister Fisk said, "and by inquiring at the Inn, I understand the horse belongs to you, sir."

The schoolmaster nodded.

"Now I have fifteen acres of wooded land, and Evans, my hired man, will need a horse to clear it. This Evans is a wiry hand, and I figure that he and a horse with a little getup about him could clear the land in a year's time."

"You would like to buy the horse?" asked Master Morgan.

"No indeed, sir. I do not wish to buy such a *little* animal. I merely wish to rent him. I stand ready to pay fifteen dollars a year, *and* his keep of course. I'll send Evans around in the morning to fetch him."

Joel was setting a log in the sawmill when he heard the cloppety-clop of hoofs coming down the river road. This in itself was nothing to make him stop work, but from the uneven beat of the hoofs he could tell that the animals were not traveling in a team. And then without

[38]

looking up at all he knew. He knew that the lighter hoofbeats were those of Little Bub. Not until he had started the saw, did he face the road.

It *was* Little Bub all right, not ten rods away. He was tied on to the back of a wagon pulled by a fat ox. His reddish coat glinted in the sunlight. And he held his head high, as if he found nothing at all disgraceful in being tied to an oxcart.

The blood hammered in Joel's head. He might have whistled and felt the hot pride of having the little horse nicker in answer. Instead, he kept murmuring the schoolmaster's words: "I've got to pay off my debts before I die. Will you gentle the colt, lad?"

Well, Bub had been gentled all right. *Any*one could see that. With a heavy heart, he watched the procession as it clattered over the log bridge and climbed up and up the steep hill. Finally it disappeared over the brow, and nothing was left of it. Nothing but a wisp of dust.

The Pulling Bee

By the time spring came on, Joel and Miller Chase were friends. In the late afternoons, while Mistress Chase napped, the miller often gave Joel a whole hour to himself.

One afternoon early in May Joel stood looking out the inn door. Suddenly the yard began filling with big-faced dray horses and oxen, and men were gathering about a huge pine log.

"Is it a pulling bee?" asked Joel, turning to Miller Chase quickly.

"If Nathan Nye is about, looking mighty important and bossy, you can be expecting most anything. He was ever good at fixing contests."

"He's there!" exclaimed Joel. "And he's got tug chains."

"H'm," mused the miller, tapping his cheek," if I was a boy now with no chores to do, it seems like I'd skedaddle right out there."

Joel grinned over his shoulder, and in no time at all he was helping Mister Nye fasten the tug chains to a big dappled mare.

The mare's owner, Abel Hooper, was too busy boasting to the farmers to be of any help. "A mighty lucky thing I'm first," he was saying. "Lucy and me'll pull this here piece a kindling to the sawmill in one pull. Then you can all hyper on home whilst it's still daylight."

But Abel Hooper had to eat his words, for Lucy barely caused the log to tremble.

One after another, the beasts had their turn, and no matter how whips cracked or masters yelled, the log seemed rooted to the earth.

"Folks, I guess it's up to the oxen now," Nathan Nye was saying, when into the yard came Evans riding Little Bub.

"Hey, Nathan," called Evans, "what's all the hullabaloo?"

"'Tis a pulling bee," answered Mister Nye, "but can't none of the beasts pull that there pine log to the sawmill in three pulls or less. Just look at Hooper's big mare! She's roaring from the try. And Biggle's gelding—his muscles are still a-hitching and a-twitching. Even Ezra Wiggins' beast failed. None of them can budge the log."

"None except my one-horse team!" crowed Evans.

Joel held his breath. He felt scared right down to his toes.

[41]

The crowd snickered. Then it hooted.

"*That* little flea? Why, he's just a sample of a horse. He ain't no bigger than a mouse's whisker! Besides, his tail is so long, he's liable to get all tangled up and break a leg."

Evans looked over the horseflesh. "Little Bub," he said slowly, "ain't exactly what you'd call a dray horse, but whatever he's hitched to generally has to come the first time trying."

"Take him on home," scoffed Nathan Nye. "When we have a contest for ponies, we'll be letting you know."

Above the man-talk Joel heard the sharp voice of Mistress Chase. "Boy! You come here!"

On his way in Joel stopped only long enough to press his face hard against Little Bub's nose.

At the door Mistress Chase handed him a kettle of hasty pudding and a long stick.

"Hang the kettle over the fire," she said, "and stir and stir until I tell you to quit."

"*Hasty* pudding!" muttered Joel to himself. "It beats me how it got its name!"

Evans strutted into the room just then. "Chase!" he called to the miller. "I'll wager a barrel of cider that my horse can move that pine log to the sawmill in two pulls. But first, pour me a mugful. I'm dying of thirst."

At sound of Evans' voice Joel almost upset the pudding.

"Boy!" shrilled Mistress Chase. "Mind your work. Hasty pudding's not meant to feed the fire!"

For once Joel paid no heed. He tore across the room and grabbed Mister Evans by the sleeve.

"Mister Evans!" he cried. "Little Bub's been dragging logs all day. You hain't going to enter him in the pulling bee?"

Evans gulped his drink. "Go away, Joel," he snapped in annoyance. "When I want advice, I'll not ask it of a whippersnapper."

The little horse meanwhile was feasting upon all the fresh green shoots within his range. They tasted juicy and delicious after the business of logging.

One by one the stars dusted the sky. Nathan Nye brought out a lanthorn so Mister Evans could see to fasten his tugchains to the log.

Joel followed Evans about like a puppy. Evans stood it as long as he could. Finally he shoved the boy aside.

"A nettle hain't half as pesky as you," he growled. "Stand back or I'll clout you."

Now Evans was stepping off the ten rods from the log to the mill.

"Want to give up before you start?" scoffed Nathan Nye.

"No such a thing. Why, I'm actually ashamed to ask my horse to pull such a little log. Now if you'll find me three stout men to sit astride the log, why then I'll ask him."

Joel bit his lips to keep from crying out. He hid his face in the horse's tangled mane. "Oh, Bub, my poor little Bub," he choked, "none of the big creatures could budge the log, and now with three men besides. Oh Bub, Bub . . ."

Laughter rang up and down the valley. "Ho-ho-ho—that pint-sized cob to pull such a big log! Ho-ho . . ."

Nathan Nye had no trouble at all in finding three brawny volunteers. As the men straddled the log, they joked and laughed and poked one another in the ribs.

"Look to your feet, men!" warned Evans. "This horse means business. Something's got to give."

Nye held the lanthorn aloft. It lighted the circle of faces. They were tense with excitement. Some of the men were placing last-minute bets with one another. Some were whittling like mad. Others twirled their whips nervously. Joel was white with anger.

Nye repeated the warning. "Look to your feet, men!"

Someone tittered.

Evans felt to see if the little horse was hitched securely. Then, "Git up!" he roared, as he slashed the whip across Bub's back.

The little horse galvanized into action. First, he backed ever so slightly. Then his powerful neck bent low, as if to give every muscle a chance to get going. Now he was straining forward. You could see his muscles grow firm and swell up like rubber balls. You could see the white foam come out on his body.

Joel, too, was drenched in sweat. The silence was heavy, like a gray blanket.

At last there was the groaning of chains. The log trembled. Slowly it moved. It kept on moving. It was more than halfway to the saw!

The little horse stopped. His sides were heaving. Joel breathed in and out with the horse. He felt as if his lungs were on fire. There was no sound at all from the crowd. Overhead a baby robin, trying to get settled for the night, chirped insistently.

Now Evans commanded again. And again the horse went through the same motions. He backed slightly. He bent his head. He strained every muscle. Again the log was moving, moving, moving. This time it did not stop until it reached the sawmill!

And still nobody had made a sound. The three men were as silent as the log they sat upon. Only the horse's breathing pierced the quiet.

[45]

Then everyone began shouting at once. "Hooray for Morgan's colt!
Hooray! Hooray! Hooray for the big-little horse."

Joel had his arms around Bub's neck. His whole body ached, as if
he had moved the log himself. "It's over! It's over! You did it, Bub!
You did it!" he kept repeating. Then he sobbed a little from exhaus-
tion and relief.

The horse lipped Joel's cheek and neck. He almost tried to say, "It's all right, Joel; don't be taking it so hard." He was steaming and tired, but it was good to be near the boy again. It was good. He nickered softly.

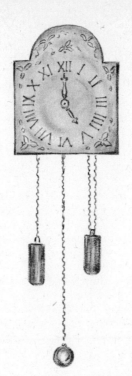

Little Bub Meets Some High-Duck Dandies

After the pulling bee Joel saw the little horse often. Nearly every week someone challenged Evans to a match, and always it was held at Chase's Inn. Word soon got around that the schoolmaster's horse could not only pull like living quicksand, but he could race the wind. Even Seth Toothaker's mare, once known as the fastest horse in the county, was defeated by the little horse.

Everywhere farmers were saying: "That creature can't be beat! 'Tis the fastest goer in all Vermont. Other horses win races by their whiskers. But not Little Bub. He's out in front the whole way."

The horse's fame spread so far that one day the mail coach from Albany, New York, pulled up to a stop right in front of the old log schoolhouse, and the driver himself handed a letter to Master Morgan. It was sealed with gold sealing wax stamped with a fancy coat of

[49]

arms, and it smelled of snuff. The handwriting was full of curlicues. In fact, although the schoolmaster was given the letter just as twilight set in, he had to wait until daylight to read it. Then he made it out as follows:

June third, 1796
NEW YORK

MY DEAR SIR:

It has come to my ears, through my good friend Ezra Fisk, that you are in possession of a horse with some ability to run. Since my partner and I have business in Brookfield, Vermont, on June the 26th, we will be glad to wager fifty dollars that our thoroughbreds—Sweepstakes and Silver Tail—will beat your horse in an eighty-rod race.

As our horses will be carrying close to 140 pounds, we must ask to have Mr. Fisk's hired man act as jockey for your horse, not the boy at Chase's Inn.

Let us meet in the Brookfield Inn at the hour of five on June the twenty-sixth.

And with a great flourish, the letter was signed,

JONATHAN FOPPINGTON, ESQUIRE

The day of the race came off fine and clear. For miles around, everyone—goldsmiths, blacksmiths, barber-surgeons, wigmakers, clockmakers, hatters, farmers—made all sorts of excuses to be in Brookfield on the day of the race. Even Master Morgan closed school at noon. And Miller Chase, in a burst of generosity, let Joel take the afternoon off.

The schoolmaster and Joel started out to walk the ten miles to Brookfield. "It seems good to be skylarking again, eh Joel?" breathed Justin Morgan. "Almost like old times. But what are you carrying in that satchel? We'll be back before midnight you know."

Joel grinned sheepishly. "It's a surprise," was all that he would say.

The schoolmaster inquired no further, for just then Lem Tubbs and his oxen, Nip and Tuck, happened along and carried them the rest of the way.

While Mister Tubbs tied his beasts to a tree, the boy and the schoolmaster entered the Brookfield Inn. There was a great bustle and stir in the gentlemen's room. Tobacco smoke lay heavy on the air. It made Joel's eyes smart, and it set the schoolmaster to coughing.

Opposite the door a little ticket window had been set up, and men with jingling silver dollars in their hands were clustered about it, waiting to place their bets. Joel watched the line. Soon he noticed, with a sinking heart, that everyone who came in after looking at Sweepstakes and Silver Tail bet *against* Little Bub.

"Hey, Morgan!" called Lem Tubbs. "Wag-on-the-wall strikes five. Where's your New Yorkers?"

All necks craned to look at the clock hanging above the mantel. With each bonging note the crowd grew quieter until there was no sound but the echo of the bell.

Then, suddenly, every nose in the room twitched. There was an unmistakable aroma of pomade. Again, as if with a single motion, all heads turned toward the stairway from which the scent came. There, mincing down the steps, as lightly as ballet dancers, tripped Jonathan Foppington and his partner. They wore ruffles of lace at their wrists, and flowered waistcoats, and their hair was powdered and curled.

When they reached the landing, both men stopped. Like actors in a play, each took a jeweled snuffbox from his waistcoat. Giving the lid three light taps, each opened his box, dipped into the snuff, and carried a dainty pinch to his nostrils. Then the men curled their lips into grotesque grins. "Ah-aah," they gasped, trying to encourage a sneeze. But no sound came. Only a sigh like that made by a bellows.

The Vermonters took their clay pipes out of their mouths and gaped. They stood so still that they might have been figures in a painting.

At last everyone began murmuring at once. Joel caught only scraps of what was said. But the remark he approved was Seth Toothaker's. "High-duck dandies I calls 'em—they and their horses, too!"

Nor did the New Yorkers try to hide *their* feelings. They looked down their noses at the Vermonters in their homespun clothes. And later, when they saw Evans come riding into the innyard, they laughed until they were red in the face.

"Egad!" they snorted. "Is this the runty little thing we've been hearing about? 'Tis almost an insult to match our noble-blooded

horses against him. Why, he's just a mongrel!" Then in a loud whisper meant for everyone to hear, the taller of the two gentlemen said, "It is a known fact that horses with short necks can't run."

This was too much for Seth Toothaker. He shook his long, horny finger and bawled out, "It may surprise you gentlemen to know that this horse hain't agoing to run with his *neck!* I and my mare, Jessie Watts, can testify to that!"

The crowd burst into a fit of laughter.

Now Nathan Nye was drawing a line across the road, and Sweepstakes was brought out from the stable behind the inn.

It was a strange pair at the starting line! One tall, satiny horse bearing a jockey in a fancy silk uniform, and one shaggy but lively work horse with a farmer on his back.

With his bulky satchel, Joel was wriggling his way up to the starting line. Carefully, he deposited the satchel on the ground. Then he undid the clasp and drew out a homely little hound-dog.

Just as Nathan Nye dropped the hat for the start of the race, Joel Goss did something he had never done before. He pinched the dog's tail as hard as ever he could. Like a streak of light the creature flew down the track, yelping loudly.

The horses were off together, but Morgan's horse shot out like an arrow. Down the track after that familiar nettlesome dog. His hind legs were drawn under him until they actually seemed to leap ahead of his front ones. His hoofs beat a quick tattoo, like the clickety music of castanets. The wind whipped at his mane and stretched out his tail until it lay level with the wind. He was not really in a race; he was flying after a noisy yelping dog.

Sweepstakes rode hard to keep up, but the distance between them was widening. The little horse was increasing his lead. He was five lengths ahead; he was ten lengths ahead. Now he and the yellow dog were crossing the finish line together! It was all Evans could do to pull him up. He had to call, "Whoa!" three times.

Joel thought he would never stop laughing. The tears rolled down his cheeks. "Hooray for Bub!" he shouted breathlessly.

The roar of the crowds sounded like thunder in the mountain. The men who lost their bets actually cheered as loud as those who won. "Did you notice?" they whooped. "He just riz up and was off like a spring freshet afore that high-duck dandy knew a race was on!"

From the corner of his eye, Joel saw the schoolmaster making his way over to him.

"Joel!" he said in a serious voice that somehow failed to match the twinkle in his eye. "Was that Abel Hooper's little yellow dog?"

"Yes, sir."

"If that was your surprise, I do not think much of it. Now round up the little dog, and we'll leave him at Mr. Hooper's on our way home."

"Yes, sir."

By this time the New Yorkers had brushed the crowd aside and were grabbing the schoolmaster's arm. Their faces were purple. "Of all the scheming tricks!" they raged, forgetting their fine manners.

Master Morgan spoke soothingly. "Gentlemen, the little dog will not interfere in the next race. I promise it."

If the race with Sweepstakes had been a victory for the little horse, the second race with Silver Tail was an even greater triumph. Silver Tail was a faster horse than Sweepstakes, and he started out to run a good race. For fifty rods he and Little Bub ran neck and neck.

On the sidelines Joel was bouncing up and down, holding imaginary reins in his hands. "Come on, Bub!" he cried. "Come on! You're eenamost there!"

It was as if the little horse had suddenly decided to get down to business. His neck strained forward, and he leaped out like a wild thing. His flinty hoofs barely touched the earth, and his legs were going so fast they blurred, like the wings of a humming bird. He inched ahead of Silver Tail, faster, faster, faster. By two lengths the little horse won.

How the crowd cheered! On all sides the shouts went up until the noise was deafening.

Silver Tail *looked* like a defeated horse. Sullen and panting, he was returned to the stables. Little Bub, however, fairly danced. He seemed to know the cheers were for him, and unashamedly he enjoyed them.

"Grit!" cried Nye. "A horse has to have grit. That's what the little creature's got. What chance had those high-duck horses, all pampered like hothouse flowers?"

It was a curious fact, but the gentlemen from New York did not try to buy Little Bub. They said he was a freak and would break down any day. Red of face, they paid their fifty dollars and disappeared into the inn. It was plain to see they wished only to get away from the jeering crowd.

On their way home in the starlight the schoolmaster and the boy, and even Lem Tubbs, were too tired to say very much. They jolted along, each one tasting his own memories. Finally Lem Tubbs turned down his lane, and Joel and Master Morgan walked the half mile into Randolph.

When almost there, the schoolmaster put out his hand and tucked five silver dollars into Joel's. Joel felt of them in wonder, tracing his finger over the eagle and the woman's head with her hair flying—like Little Bub's he thought. He had seen plenty of silver dollars at the inn, but these were the first he had ever held for his own. "Do you know," he said with a little sigh of happiness, "I reckon now I can buy Little Bub when I'm of age. Miller Chase has promised to give me two suits of clothes then, but I aim to ask for the money instead. And with these dollars besides, why I'll be able to buy Bub as easy as anything!"

"He'll be very old then, lad, and you'll be man-grown."

Joel only half heard. It never occurred to him that Little Bub would some day be an old horse. The years ahead seemed like nothing. Nothing at all. In just a short time he would own the fastest horse in Vermont!

"Things are working out fine, Master Morgan!" and he reached in his satchel to pat the little hound-dog because he felt good toward the whole wide world.

"Things are working out fine for me, too, Joel. I can pay my debts now—to the very last dollar!"

They walked on in silence, each remembering that early morning when Little Bub turned out of Farmer Beane's gate and came along uninvited.

Little Bub
Preserves a Name

By autumn Little Bub's year of rental was up, and he was returned to Justin Morgan.

Scarcely had Evans turned over the reins when horse-trader Hawkes, and many others, came knocking at the schoolmaster's door. They hemmed and hawed to hide their feelings, but it was plain that they were greedy for the little horse. They began outbidding each other until one afternoon the talk drifting out of the schoolhouse sounded as if an auction were going on.

The schoolmaster could not help smiling, but he shook his head to all offers. "I do not need the money, gentlemen," he said. "My debts are all paid, except to a lad named Joel. If I use the horse gently, he *may* live long enough to pay that debt, too. Meanwhile Bub can carry me around on my singing circuit. My legs are not as stout as they used to be."

Thus began, for Little Bub, a life of joyful ease. While Master Morgan gave singing lessons he was not even tied to a hitching post. The schoolyard was his! He could gallop around and around with all the wild freedom of his colthood. Often, after a good hard run, he would drop down on the cool grass and roll back and forth, his feet pawing the sky. Sometimes white dandelion blowballs would tickle his nos-

trils. Then he bugled through his nose and snorted and sneezed them away. But when the wind was still he, too, lay still, just listening to the children sing the hymns that his master composed.

The moment he heard the scuffling of feet in the cloakroom, however, he was up in a flash and waiting at the schoolhouse door. As the children came tumbling out, they gave him pieces of horehound candy or apples from their dinner pails.

Bub's school days were all too short. One morning Justin Morgan felt too ill to teach, and the very next day he left for Woodstock, Vermont, taking the horse with him.

Always now Joel watched the mail coach for a letter. After months of waiting it appeared all of a sudden in Mistress Chase's hands one early morning. She was holding it against the candlelight when Joel came down to rake aside the ashes and kindle the fire.

"Never knew a letter to bring *good* news," she snapped," and poor news means poor work. Time enough to read this when your day's work is done."

Then she flung the letter on the bar counter where strangers would be fingering it all day long. And all day long she eyed Joel like a cat waiting for a mouse to make one false move.

It was after dark when Joel hung up his leather apron and raced up the ladder steps to his room, clutching the letter in his hand. By the flickering light of the candle, he pored over each word.

JOEL LAD:

The Rice family here in Woodstock have been caring for me during my long illness, and once again I am in debt. I know you will understand if I leave our horse to them. He is in fine fettle, lad, round-barreled and glossy.

Somehow, sometime you will find a way to take care of Little Bub. May that day come soon, because only then will you and he be content.

Meanwhile I send you my songbooks. If my last pilgrimage be as pleasant as the one with you and the colts, I shall be happy. Good-by, and God bless you.

I am, dear Joel,

Your friend always,
JUSTIN MORGAN

WOODSTOCK, VERMONT
February 27, 1798

Joel memorized the letter. Then he folded it around his five silver dollars, tied it in his handkerchief, and tucked the handkerchief beneath his straw bedtick.

No one knew quite how it happened, but after Justin Morgan died, his name was given to the little horse. When Joel heard about this he was glad.

"The schoolmaster would be proud to fasten his name on Little Bub," he said.

In the years that followed, the Morgan horse went from one master to another. He served blacksmiths and farmers, bricklayers and carpenters, and they all used him hard. By day he hauled lumber and bricks. He uprooted stumps. He dragged logs and stones. He cultivated the land. But at night, with the mud brushed from his coat, he cantered into town with as much snap and style as any carriage horse.

What amazed everyone was that instead of growing thin and poor, the little horse grew tough and strong. He seemed to work for the *fun* of working. It was as if he liked the clanking jingle of tug chains, the creaking of sledge runners over frozen snow, the smell of freshly turned earth. In all Vermont there was not another horse so vigorous, so full of spirit, yet so gentle. Powerful enough to please the men, he was also docile enough to carry the most delicate lady to a quilting party. And when a neighbor had a house-raising or a chopping bee, the owner of the Morgan horse was first to be invited!

Now, each time he was up for sale, the price mounted higher and higher until Joel's five dollars seemed to shrink and shrivel like bacon

over a hot fire. Even if Joel could have borrowed the money, he had nowhere to keep a horse.

At these sales Justin Morgan often caught the smell of the boy or heard his voice. Then, how he whickered for joy and how he reached out with his nose to gather in the familiar scent. Joel would be at his side in an instant. "Listen Justin," he would whisper into the quivering ears, "next time I'll have a whole pocketful of money. You see if I don't! And I'll give you a green meadow with a creek snakin' through it. Think of that! And I'll give you a fine stable with a thick bed of straw. And I'll give you sweet hay, and all the oats you can eat. And I'll give you a blanket in winter. And I'll rub you proper night and morning." Then, when he could think of nothing more to give, he would run his strong young hands over the horse's muscles. And, if no one happened to be looking, he would feel his own muscles.

"Hard as flint," he would laugh, "yes, 'tis just as I said! You and me *are* growing big together."

Joel was doing a man's work now. His years of apprenticeship were almost over. He worked with a fierce joy, knowing that soon he would have a mill of his own; and he would raise colts on the side, and they would all be Morgan colts. What did it matter if, in the midst of such happy dreams, Mistress Chase snapped a dish towel smartly across his face and gave her opinion of apprentices who had only half a mind on their work? Joel neither felt the sting of the towel nor the sting of the words, for in a few days the long years would be up.

Then an unbelievable thing happened. Justin Morgan was sold to a traveler, and man and horse dropped out of sight as completely as if they had been swallowed by quicksand. *No* one seemed to have any knowledge of the new owner.

Desperately, Joel attended every county fair and farm auction. Almost daily he questioned Trader Hawkes until the man would hide behind a cart or a bale of hay to avoid the boy's eyes. He worried Evans, too, and Mister Fisk and Mister Rice. He even wrote Jonathan Foppington of New York.

He stopped every guest at Chase's Inn and carefully described the horse. "Reddish-brown," he would say pridefully, "with a great wide space between the eyes, and ears that prick forward, and he's only about fourteen hands high, but he's *big* for his size."

Always the answer was the same, "Sorry, young feller. I call to mind plenty of big beasts, but no such little cob."

Days stretched out into years. War came. The War of 1812 it was called. And no one was the least bit surprised when Joel enlisted in the cavalry instead of the infantry.

But even the business of war did not end Joel's search. When he realized that Justin Morgan was not among the horses in his division, he asked to join the scouting troops patrolling the Niagara border. There he saw many blooded English horses, but no short-legged little horse with a proud free spirit.

"This be a half-hearted war!" Joel often complained to Timothy Tubbs, a drummer boy from Randolph. "I'd as lief do some hard fighting or else stayed to home."

In the full heat of the battle of Lundy's Lane, Joel could not help remembering that his wish had come startlingly true. All the long night of July 25, 1814, he and his mount were bringing up gunpowder and moving cannon. Just when the battery fell to the Americans, Colonel Ripley sent Joel to help the medical aides. They improvised stretchers out of coats by thrusting muskets through the sleeves.

[65]

By morning the wounded had been moved to hospital tents. But still Joel could not give way to his own weariness. What if one of the horses lying in Lundy's Lane were Justin Morgan?

He worked quickly now. He filled an empty powder horn with alum and went to the horses.

A veterinarian was already on the field. "Handle the flesh wounds," he ordered. "I'll take the bad ones."

Joel tried not to hear the screams of the horses. He was glad for the roaring of Niagara Falls. With steady hand he poured the alum into open wounds. All the time he talked to the terrified animals as if they were small children in trouble.

"I declare!" said the veterinarian later. "It puzzled me if 'twas the alum or your voice that stopped the blood and the screaming."

Long afterward Joel was not certain whether he was glad or sorry that Justin Morgan was not among the wounded of Lundy's Lane.

A Whinny in the Night

After the battle of Lundy's Lane the war began to peter out. Both America and England suddenly realized that they had nothing to fight about. With Napoleon captured and the fighting at an end in Europe, the very reasons for the war disappeared. So the whole business was called off. It was almost as simple as that. There were no harsh terms for either side to carry out. Nothing but blessed peace.

News of the peace brought great rejoicing. The blockade along the Atlantic coast was lifted. The country began to build a great merchant marine. Men began dreaming of free public schools, of clean prisons, of putting an end to slavery.

And in the little town of Randolph, Vermont, progress was also afoot. Joel, man-grown now, was an important member of the community. Even white-bearded old men nodded and smiled when his name was said.

One wintry night, in the year 1817, Joel was on his way to the meetinghouse to discuss the opening of a library in some parishioner's home. With his skates over his shoulder he stopped to pick up Timothy Tubbs.

Usually the two men talked and laughed as they skated up the river to the meetinghouse. But not this night. The wind howled and whined like a trapped animal, and a fine dry snow pricked their faces like so many needle points.

Suddenly as they rounded the bend of the river, Joel heard a horse whinny. It was not an ordinary whinny. Even above the wind he caught the short high note, and then a low, but distinct, rumble. The sound seemed to come from somewhere in the direction of Chase's Inn.

Joel spun around so quickly that he sent Timothy sprawling across the ice.

"So help me, Timothy!" he cried. "Seems as though I've heard that particular neigh before."

"Likely you have!" replied Timothy as he rescued his cap, which had been neatly lifted off his head by the long finger of a willow branch. "Likely you have, but is that a fit reason for trying to break every bone in my body?"

Joel made no answer. His ears were tuned to the neighing of a horse. Breathlessly he scrambled up the river bank, the hard crust of snow creaking under his weight.

In an instant he was in the familiar shed behind the inn. Ripping off his skates, he took the lanthorn that hung over the entrance and went from stall to stall, lighting the faces of the animals.

A white face. An iron-gray face. A black face. A dappled face. Then a broad-faced ox. Some of the animals had white stripes down their noses. Some had no marks at all. But in all the long row there was not a single reddish-brown face with lively, intelligent eyes.

Sick with disappointment, Joel returned the lanthorn to its peg. But again that short, high note cut the frosty air. And again the low rumble died away. This time the sound seemed to come from in front of the inn. With Timothy at his heels, Joel flew across the innyard. And there, tied to the block, stood a team of six horses hitched to a huge freight wagon.

Joel stopped stock still. These horses were miserable and old. There was not a proud head nor a beautiful arched neck among them. Suddenly the neighing began again. Now Joel was close enough to see which horse moved.

His heart seemed to stop altogether, then began beating wildly. "So help me!" he breathed. "'Tis the littlest horse in the team. 'Tis Justin Morgan! That's who 'tis—Justin Morgan!"

In a flash he was holding the horse's face in his hands, caressing his nose and combing the matted forelock with his fingers. He tried to thaw the tiny icicles that clung to the horse's whiskers. "My poor Little Bub!" he whispered softly. "My poor, shivering, frightened Little Bub, with his ribs a-sticking out like barrel staves!"

The little horse was trembling—not from the cold, but from joy. He tried to nicker, but all he could manage was a whimper. It was as if he had spent himself in neighing and now wanted only to rest his head in Joel's hands. He nuzzled them feebly.

"Look Joel! Look at the signboard!" called Timothy, laughing heartily.

Above the horses, the signboard swung back and forth, creaking on its hinges. The last line, only a few inches above the shivering team, read, "Good Keeping for Horses."

Joel's eyes seemed to strike sparks in the cold. "It hain't going to be easy," he said, "to make you understand about this little horse. But when I knew him he could walk faster, run faster, and pull heavier logs than any horse in Vermont! 'Tis the Justin Morgan horse, Timothy! 'Tis the Justin Morgan horse, I tell you!"

"This old beast the singing master's horse?" gasped Timothy.

"The very one."

Now Timothy seemed as interested as Joel. He felt of the horse's bony sides. "The creature's wore a harness so long 'tis a wonder it ain't grown on him," he said. "Well, what in thunder we waiting for?"

At least a dozen men were at the bar counter of the inn when Joel and Timothy entered.

"Gentlemen!" Joel addressed them, in a calm, strong voice he scarcely knew as his own. "Who owns the six-horse team at the hitching block?"

"I do!" snarled a harsh voice from behind a high-backed rocker. "And what's it to you?"

From where Joel and Timothy stood, all they could see was the back of the rocker, with two enormous feet showing beyond it. The feet were stretched toward the hearth, where a wood fire blazed and crackled.

Joel and Timothy made their way over to the teamster who sat comfortably rocking back and forth. His face was half-hidden behind a red beard, and his almost-yellow eyes stared straight ahead, like those of a horned owl. He fitted so snugly between the arms of the rocker that

[71]

Joel could not help wondering how he would ever get out. Across his lap lay a bullhide whip, and in one hand he held a steaming tankard of punch. As he waved the two men to chairs, the punch spattered until some of it struck the fire with a loud hiss.

Joel and Timothy sat down, one on either side of the teamster. Then taking a deep breath as if he were about to dive into an icy stream, Joel blurted out, "How much do you want for the littlest horse in your team?"

The man's eyes narrowed until they were thin slits. He wondered if his ears were playing him tricks. Surely this greenhorn could not have meant the *littlest* horse. But yes, he was repeating the question, louder this time.

It was all the teamster could do not to laugh aloud. Why, only today he had been wondering how soon he would have to sell the old beast for just his hide alone! And now someone was preparing to offer hard money for him.

He shook his head as if that might make him think clearer. With an effort he leaned forward and placed the whip and his tankard on the floor. Then he stared into the fire, his yellow eyes matching the flames.

"Young feller," he said, combing his beard with his fingers, "that little fellow can pull better than all the clodhoppers in the team put together. I wouldn't *hear* of selling him nowise! Why, 'twas less than a fortnight ago I turned down twenty dollars for him!"

Joel called Miller Chase aside. "Sir," he said earnestly, "ever since I was a little tyke, I've hankered for the Morgan horse. Now he's right here in the innyard, and if I don't buy him tonight, sir, he may be dead in the morning."

Miller Chase did not answer at once, but there was a kindliness in his eyes.

"Joel lad," he said at last," you have your own sawmill now, and you may be an old man by the time it's paid for. Times are awful hard. What's the sense of getting deeper in debt on a nearly dead beast? The Morgan horse must be in his twenties, and any horse that old is liable to be rheumaticky and die soon."

"Yes, yes, I know," spoke Joel impatiently. "But this horse is different, sir. He's a friend, and you don't turn down a friend just because he's old."

The miller smiled. And then as he caught sight of Mistress Chase he lowered his voice to a whisper. "All right, son," he said. "I'll loan you whatever it takes."

Justin Morgan and the President of the United States

No human patient ever received more tender care than did the little horse. Joel prepared warm mashes of oats, thinned with linseed tea, to coax his appetite. At first he ate only to please Joel. Each swallow was a painful effort. But in a week or two he was eating because he could not help himself.

Oh, how good everything tasted! Delicious hay, so sweet-smelling that it stirred up memories of green meadows. Corn and oats ground in Joel's own gristmill. Carrots and apples and rutabagas chopped fine. And rock salt in the manger where he could lick it a dozen times a day.

Even the water was strength-giving. The teamster expected his horses to eat snow for water, or to break ice in a stream. But Joel Goss not only provided fresh water; he enriched it with oatmeal.

In every move of Joel's there was life-giving warmth: warmth in the rubdowns with Joel's woolen mittens, in the soft flannel bandages that Joel wrapped about his legs, in the melted wool fat with which Joel bathed the cracks in his feet, in the homespun blanket with which Joel tenderly covered him, and warmth in the thick bed of straw on which to lie.

It was like magic the way Justin Morgan responded! His body grew round. His eyes became lively and lustrous again. Once more he held his head high. All Randolph was saying, "I declare the little horse is as spry as a grasshopper!"

One fine July morning—July 24, 1817, to be exact—there was a special kind of excitement in the air. In a stable in Burlington, Vermont, Joel was brushing and polishing Justin Morgan as if his life de-

pended on it. It made the horse feel frisky as a colt. He had never been groomed this carefully. Why, each lock of his hair was being brushed separately!

With a final pat on Justin's nose, Joel drew the horse's head close to him. "Listen, Justin," he whispered into the twitching ears, "in an hour you and I are going to be in a parade, and the President of the United States will be there!

"Do you know," he added softly, "you're just naturally growing young. Your heart be young and so be you. I bet there hain't a finer horse in all the nineteen states!"

An hour later Joel and his horse were swinging into formation. Joel was wearing his cavalry uniform. The green coat with its white facings and the white breeches had been cleaned and patched until they looked almost as good as new. And he wore a sprig of evergreen in his helmet to show that he was one of the Green Mountain boys.

Every now and again Joel flushed when a breeze fluttered the blue ribbon pinned on his chest and the sun picked out the gold letters that spelled "Battle of Lundy's Lane."

There were young boys and old men in the division of cavalry in which Joel was riding. And there were fine military horses and some that looked as if they had just come from their work in the fields. But to Joel, none had the gallant spirit of Justin Morgan.

Oh, the joy of having the little horse for his own! He obeyed the lightest pressure of Joel's knees. He seemed to know what Joel wanted even before the signal was given. He formed in line obediently. He marched smoothly. He walked backward. He walked sideways. Proudly he kept time to the beat of the drums. In all the long procession there was no finer parade horse.

At the command of "Halt!" a number of animals pawed the ground, and many switched their tails. But Justin Morgan stood as still as the statue which was later made of him. Even when a salute of guns was fired from the battery, and some of the horses tried to bolt, the Morgan horse never flinched.

Now from every church steeple, bells began to ring—softly at first, then louder and louder until the sound seemed to roll out in great waves.

When at last the bells were stilled there was no sound in all the great gathering until a schoolmaster, who stood on a little platform, raised a wooden pitchpipe to his lips. Timidly he set the tune for that new song, "The Star Spangled Banner." It was as if that thin sound had touched off a cannon. Two hundred school children had been waiting overlong for this very signal. At the top of their lungs, they sang out,

> O say, can you see,
> By the dawn's early light,
> What so proudly we hailed
> At the twilight's last gleaming? . . .

At exactly the moment when the song was over, a deep voice boomed, "Ladies and gentlemen, the President of the United States!" Then James Monroe himself was escorted between the rows of men mounted on horseback. He proceeded slowly until he came to Justin Morgan. Then he stopped. He looked at the horse with admiration. He motioned to have him brought forward out of line.

Joel Goss jumped down and handed the reins to the President of the United States while a little murmur of surprise rippled down the lines like a small breeze stirring a row of flower heads.

The little horse seemed to understand the greatness of the occasion. He allowed the President to mount with ease. Then he stood tall, his nostrils quivering. Something seemed to stir within him. For one brief instant his eyes took on a faraway look. He might have been thinking of his lifetime of toil, the tree stumps he had pulled, the years in a six-horse team. Then his eyes flashed as if, in this moment, the hardships had all been washed away. He whickered lightly.

When the parade reached College Hill, the President dismounted, and, with one hand resting lightly on Morgan's saddle, he made a speech. He said that no nation had a richer treasure than LIBERTY. And he was proud of the way American liberty had been defended by the Green Mountain Boys. The people of Vermont, he said, are as firm as the mountains that gave them birth. They have preserved the highest honor of the country.

The crowds cheered and threw their hats into the air. The President bowed. Justin Morgan bowed, too. The crowds went wild. It was hard to tell whether the President of the United States or the little horse was the hero of the day!

The parade over, people came swarming around Joel and his horse. Boys and girls, men and women, fumbled in homespun pockets and bags for good things to eat. They all wanted to go home and say, "I eenamost touched the President of the United States, but I actually did feed the horse he swung up on!"

Some of the very farmers who had once poked fun at the Morgan's long tail were now trying to snip a few hairs from it for a souvenir. "I always knew he would be a go-ahead horse!" they crowed.

Those who were honest said, "And I can remember when School-master Morgan couldn't sell the creature nohow. And here he's out-lived two horses!"

"Fellers," nodded one very old man, "I more than half believe the Morgan horse is human."

Who *is* the Justin Morgan horse? Who was his sire? Who was his dam?

Over mugs of cider in the Burlington inn, questions popped like sparks from a dry log. In the midst of them a white-bearded man banged his mug on the table to silence the crowd.

"Maybe you folks be too young to remember," he spat, "but one black night during the Revolutionary War a fancy English thorough-bred of the name of True Briton was hitched at a tavern near the British lines. Then along come a Yankee and what did he do?"

"What?" chorused the crowd.

"Why, he stole that there British horse and raced him across the lines. And 'twas him that fathered Justin Morgan! The mare was a lively Arabian of the Wild Air breed."

"Sorry to contradict you, grandpap," Lem Tubbs broke in apolo-getically, "but I and the schoolmaster was close friends, and he always said his horse was a Dutch horse."

"Lem, you're as wrong as a pump without a handle!" chirped a little cricket of a man. "'Twas the singing master himself owned the mother of Justin Morgan! The sire was a French-Canadian horse."

"Begging your pardon," interrupted the innkeeper. "'Twas True Briton the schoolmaster owned, *not* the mare."

The talk seesawed back and forth—first about little Morgan's parents, then about his birthday. Some said he was foaled in 1789. Some insisted it was 1793.

In the heat of the arguing, the door opened and Major Brinsmaid, who had directed the parade, strode into the room. He had with him a cavalryman who was flushed to the roots of his stubbly hair. It was none other than Joel Goss.

The crowd in the inn stood.

"At ease, gentlemen," smiled the major. "Word has reached me that you want to know about the Morgan horse. Here, my friends, is the man who can tell you."

A great silence came over the gathering as all eyes turned toward Joel who would rather have fought a dozen battles than speak.

At last he cleared his throat. "Like as not you folks know as much as I do about the Morgan horse," he explained with a little smile. "I was just a spindling youngster when the schoolmaster and I went down to Farmer Beane's of West Springfield, Massachusetts, to collect a debt owing the master. Farmer Beane just didn't have the money, but he was not a man to be beholden to anyone. He allowed that Ebenezer, a fine big colt of his, would more than settle things. And for good measure, he even threw in a short-legged colt called Little Bub.

"Nobody set much store by Little Bub; that is, not at first. Yet it was him that paid off the debt!"

[83]

Joel stopped, but it was plain that the people wanted to hear more. "The schoolmaster and Farmer Beane are both dead now," he went on slowly, thoughtfully, "and likely nobody will ever know who was the little colt's father and who was his mother. He was just a little work horse that cleared the fields and helped Vermont grow up."

Then suddenly Joel's face lit up as if he had just thought of something for the first time. "Why, come to think of it, he's like us. He's American, that's what he is. American!"

The Heart to Go on Forever

The story of Justin Morgan has not ended. The brave little horse lives on. He had many colts. Six or twelve, or fourteen. Maybe more.

His children, too, had many children. This in itself is not remarkable. But it was exceedingly remarkable that all of the grandchildren should look like Justin Morgan. Carbon copies one might say. They all had the wonderfully proud heads with that wide space between the eyes. They all had the same round-barreled bodies and the short, sturdy legs. And they all had deep chests with ample room for powerful lungs and the Morgan heart. What is more, they all traveled with the same easy grace. Even when they were little foals, it was plain to see that Justin Morgan was the image from which they were made.

The likeness did not stop with looks. It went deeper. Justin Morgan's grandchildren inherited an inner something. Men gave it various names. Courage. Power. Intelligence. The heart to go on forever. Some called it a high free spirit and let it go at that. One driver who carried the mail before the days of the railroad said, "Through blinding sleet and heavy drifts, I never had a Morgan horse look back to refuse me. They always faced the blast. If a double trip had to be made, the Morgans were the ones to do it."

[85]

No less than forty descendants of Justin Morgan became famous as trotters. Ethan Allen, Black Hawk, and Cock of the Rock made trotting history. And Dan Patch, who inherited strong Morgan characteristics, set the mile record for pacing, a record which stood for thirty-three years.

Morgans also became the war horses of America. General Custer rode a Morgan horse when he went off to fight the Indians. And in the War Between the States a whole regiment was mounted on Morgans. "It was your *horses* licked us!" a southerner admitted. One of these horses, Rienzi, was ridden by General Sheridan when he hastened to defend the city of Washington. And the ride has gone down in history:

> Be it said in letters bold and bright:
> "Here is the steed that saved the day
> By carrying Sheridan into the fight
> From Winchester, twenty miles away!"

Today Morgan horses are making good as police horses of our great cities, as cow ponies of the western plains, and as business and pleasure horses in nearly every country in the world. In fact, wherever a spirited but gentle "go-ahead horse" is wanted, a Morgan is the answer. Today Morgan horses are taking blue ribbons at horse shows and stock exhibitions, and the name Morgan means something—like *all-wool* or the sterling mark on silver. Justin Morgan himself would probably be proud to know that wherever farms are hilly, farm machinery has never replaced the Morgan, and probably never will.

Vermont people do not forget. To them, the name Morgan is part of their heritage. Like the Green Mountains. Or the winding rivers.

[86]

In 1939 Vermont lawmakers passed a resolution to celebrate the one hundred and fiftieth anniversary of Justin Morgan's birth. The resolution was read before the entire state assembly. It was full of whereases and big words, but it simply meant this:

Since Justin Morgan brought fame and wealth to Vermont, and since his colts helped to build so many American breeds of light horses, something ought to be done to celebrate his birthday.

And so, a man from the Senate and two men from the House of Representatives did something about it. They arranged to have prizes for Morgan horses at the Fall Horse Shows that year, and they sent true stories about Justin Morgan's life to the newspapers. It was all a glowing tribute to a little reddish-brown stallion with a high free spirit.

But perhaps the greatest tribute of all is a living one. In the tiny Vermont village of Weybridge, the United States Department of Agriculture has a Morgan Horse Farm. In all America it is the only farm founded so that one breed of horses shall live forever.

At the entrance gate to the farm stands a life-size bronze statue of Justin Morgan. Proud history lives in the simple inscription: the history of a common ordinary little work horse which turned out to be the father of a great breed of American horses; the history of a gallant little horse that blazed a trail in the wilderness and helped build a new nation; the history of Justin Morgan, pioneer American.

FOR THEIR HELP THE AUTHOR IS GRATEFUL TO

WALTER B. MAHONY, great-great-grandson of Justin Morgan · FANNIE S. GOSS, granddaughter of Joel Goss · F. B. HILLS, Secretary, The Morgan Horse Club · Vermont Historical Society · DR. PAUL O. McGREW, Chicago Natural History Museum · HELEN HARTNESS FLANDERS, Archivist for Vermont Traditional Music · The Chicago Public Library · Fletcher Free Library, Burlington, Vermont · St. Johnsbury Athenaeum, St. Johnsbury, Vermont · The Library of the University of Vermont · State of Vermont Reference Bureau at Montpelier · Fiske Foundation Library, Claremont, New Hampshire · DR. C. J. ATTIG, Head of History, North Central College · The late DAVID DANA HEWITT, Vermont pioneer

1921
GIVEN BY THE MORGAN HORSE CLUB
TO THE
U. S. DEPARTMENT OF AGRICULTURE
IN MEMORY OF
JUSTIN MORGAN WHO DIED IN
1821

WESLEY DENNIS·